DREAMWORKS
GABBY'S DOLLHOUSE

CatRat's BIRTHDAY Surprise

Adapted by Pamela Bobowicz

DreamWorks Gabby's Dollhouse © 2024 DreamWorks Animation LLC. All Rights Reserved.

All rights reserved. Published by Scholastic Inc., *Publishers since 1920.* SCHOLASTIC and associated logos are trademarks and/or registered trademarks of Scholastic Inc.

The publisher does not have any control over and does not assume any responsibility for author or third-party websites or their content.

No part of this publication may be reproduced, stored in a retrieval system, or transmitted in any form or by any means, electronic, mechanical, photocopying, recording, or otherwise, without written permission of the publisher. For information regarding permission, write to Scholastic Inc., Attention: Permissions Department, 557 Broadway, New York, NY 10012.

This book is a work of fiction. Names, characters, places, and incidents are either the product of the author's imagination or are used fictitiously, and any resemblance to actual persons, living or dead, business establishments, events, or locales is entirely coincidental.

ISBN 978-1-339-04951-9

10 9 8 7 6 5 4 3 2 1   24 25 26 27 28

Printed in the U.S.A.   40

First printing 2024

Book design by Salena Mahina and Stacie Zucker

Scholastic Inc.

I have a surprise for Floyd! I made him a pawsome new toy. I hope he likes it!

Meow! Meow! Meow! Meow!

You know what that sound means! It's time for a Dollhouse Delivery!

Today's Kitty Cat Surprise Box looks like CatRat! It's a special birthday delivery.

I know! We should throw CatRat a surprise party. Would you like to join us?

We'll need a cake, decorations, and a super surprise guest.

I'll invite CatRat's favorite rock-star kitty—Fluffy Flufferton.
She and DJ Catnip can sing a special surprise song.

There is a lot to do today. It's time to get tiny!

Welcome to the dollhouse!

"Guess what today is," I say to Cakey.

"What?" Cakey asks.

"It's CatRat's birthday!"

The first thing we need for a super surprise birthday is a super surprise birthday cake!

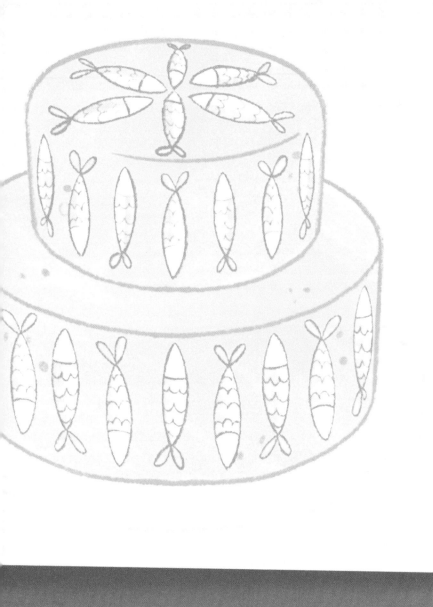

"Sprinkle-rific! I know just the thing!" Cakey says.
"A sardine upside-down cake. It's CatRat's favorite!"

Cakey tells Pandy and me that the most important part of an upside-down cake is you have to bake it upside down!

We flip upside down and stay like that until the cake is done. Meow-mazing!

The cake's done! It's time to decorate it to look like CatRat.

"We can't forget a birthday smile!" Cakey says.

Oh no! I think I hear CatRat coming. We've got to hide the cake and the baking stuff!

CatRat appears. "I thought I smelled something . . . birthday cakey," CatRat says.

Oh no! I have to distract him.

"It's National Hug a Cat Day!" I say.

When CatRat leaves, I ask Cakey to find an even more secret hiding place for the cake until it's time for the party.

Now it's time to make some decorations with Baby Box. To the craft room!

Baby Box and her brothers are excited to help.

Baby Box thinks CatRat will like a shiny birthday crown.

"CatRat can be king for the day!" I say.

The Box brothers make some sparkling cup lights to decorate.

They even add sardines, just for CatRat!

CatRat surprises us when he enters the craft room.

"Looks like someone's been doing a little crafting," CatRat says. "Making something special for anyone I know?"

We can't let CatRat guess the surprise!

"Um, we were celebrating National . . . Cutty Cutty Day," I say.

"You mean today is National Hug a Cat Day *and* National Cutty Cutty Day?" CatRat asks. He looks sad. We can't keep this secret much longer.

After CatRat leaves, I say, "We've got to make sure CatRat knows we didn't forget his birthday!"

Ring! It's Fluffy Flufferton!

She's in the music room with DJ Catnip. They need our help!

We're on our way!

In the music room, Fluffy and DJ Catnip are writing their birthday song. The words don't rhyme . . . yet!

We work together to make a great song.

It's party time! Everyone is here.

"The room looks a-meow-zing!" I say.

"Quick, everyone, hide! It's time for CatRat's birthday surprise!"

SURPRISE!

"Wow!" CatRat says. "A surprise party? For me?"

We shout, "Happy birthday, CatRat!"

CatRat loves his birthday crown, his cake, and all the decorations!

But best of all, he loves his birthday song sung by Fluffy, DJ Catnip, and all his friends!

"With friends like you, I already have the best present in the world," CatRat says. "This is the best birthday ever!"

Our super surprise birthday was a super success! Thanks for joining us! Happy birthday, CatRat!